To my mother

Day in, day out, Ruby did the same old stuff.

"What a hum-drum life," she complained.

Story and Pictures by Amy Aitken

Bradbury Press Scarsdale, New York

J
A

3 2 1 81 80 79
The text of this book is set in 18 pt. Caledonia. The illustrations are pencil and watercolor wash, reproduced in full color.

Library of Congress Cataloging in Publication Data
Aitken, Amy. Ruby!
Summary: Anything is possible for Ruby. She decides to be an author or an artist or a movie star or maybe even President.
[1. Occupations—Fiction] I. Title.
PZ7.A2836Ru [E] 78-21283
ISBN 0-87888-144-1

One morning, Ruby was reading a book she had borrowed from her friend Axel.

"What a stupid story," Ruby said to herself. "I could write a better book than this. I think I will, too!"

"I'm going to write a book," she told her mother. "Everyone will read it. I'll be famous overnight!"

"I thought you wanted to be a rock star," her mother said.

"Not anymore," said Ruby.

Ruby went out to find Axel and tell him her new plan.

"Soon I won't be able to walk down the street without being recognized," she thought.

EXTRA!
RUBY'S IN TOWN!
WALKS DOWN BLOCK

RTV

"Hey Ruby," someone said. "Want to go to the park?"

It was Axel.

"No," said Ruby. "I'm going to write a book."

"What about being a rock star," said Axel. "I was going to be your drummer."

"You can help me write the book," Ruby said. "Your handwriting is neater."

"What kind of book?" Axel asked.

"A very long one," said Ruby. "With a red cover. I'll be famous, of course. Want my autograph now?"

"I can wait," said Axel.

"First, let's have something to eat," Ruby said. "It's impossible to write on an empty stomach."

They went inside and made peanut butter and jelly sandwiches.

"That was good," said Axel. "Let's have another."

"Okay," Ruby said. "Soon I won't have time to eat. I'll be much too busy flying around the world."

They took their sandwiches into Ruby's room.

"Now I'm going to write my masterpiece," said Ruby.

"Afterwards, let's go to the park," said Axel.

"Quiet! I'm concentrating."

At the top of the page Ruby wrote, 'A BOOK, by Ruby.' She drew a little picture of herself.

"Hey! Look at this drawing!" said Ruby.

"What about it?"

"I'm an artist!" Ruby cried. "And here I've been wasting my time writing books. Artists lead a much more exciting life."

RUBY'S
PAINTING
OF AXEL!

"Want to go to the park now?" asked Axel.

"Don't move!" Ruby said. "I'm going to paint your portrait. People will travel far and wide to see it!"

Ruby found her paints under the bed.

"Uh-oh," she said. "No more blue. How will I paint your blue eyes?"

"I have blue at my house," said Axel. "I'll go get it."

"Hurry up," said Ruby.

While Axel was gone, Ruby thought about being an artist.

"My painting will make newspaper headlines. In fact, someone will probably make a movie about me!"

"Of course!" she cried, "I'll be a movie star!"

RUBY
RUBY
DIRECTOR

RUBY
REVUE

"Wait until Axel hears about this!"

She rushed outside, just as Axel was coming up.

"Is there a fire?" Axel gasped.

"I am going to be a movie star," Ruby announced.

"But what about my portrait?"

"You can be my leading man," said Ruby. "A movie, starring Ruby and Axel!"

"Now do you want to go to the park?" Axel asked.

"Okay," said Ruby. "After all, we'll be too busy to play when we're movie stars. Everyone will want our autographs."

"Even the President?"

"Of course."

"Come to think of it," Ruby thought, "I always wanted to be President."

ELECT
RUBY
GO-GO
RUBY